06-02

Easy V

MARCIA VAUGHAN

Illustrated by *Ann Schweninger*

We're Going on a Ghost Hunt

Silver Whistle
Harcourt, Inc.
San Diego
New York
London

For Rosemary Stimola, one sharp cookie!
—M. V.

For Maggie Byer-Sprinzeles
—A. S.

www.harcourt.com

Silver Whistle is a trademark of Harcourt, Inc., registered in the United States of America and/or other jurisdictions.

Library of Congress Cataloging-in-Publication Data
Vaughan, Marcia K.
We're going on a ghost hunt/Marcia Vaughan; illustrated by Ann Schweninger.—1st ed.
p. cm.
"Silver Whistle."
Summary: When trick-or-treaters let their imaginations run wild, ordinary backyard items seem spooky, so that a mud puddle looks like a swamp and tree branches look like skeletons.
[1. Ghosts—Fiction. 2. Halloween—Fiction. 3. Stories in rhyme.] I. Schweninger, Ann, ill. II. Title.
PZ8.3.V71256We 2001
[E]—dc21 99-50729
ISBN 0-15-202353-4

First edition
H G F E D C B A

Printed in Singapore

The illustrations in this book were created in linoleum cut, then printed with oil base block-printing ink and enhanced with watercolor paint.
The display type was set in Bernhard Antique.
The text type was set in Minion Semibold.
Color separations by Bright Arts Ltd., Hong Kong
Printed and bound by Tien Wah Press, Singapore
This book was printed on totally chlorine-free Nymolla Matte Art paper.
Production supervision by Sandra Grebenar and Ginger Boyer
Designed by Linda Lockowitz

Do you want to go on a ghost hunt
to catch a trick-or-treat ghost?
We're not afraid.
No, we're not afraid.
No, we're not afraid at all!

Looking high.
Looking low.
Off on a ghost hunt.
Here we go!

Oh, dear. What have we here?
A swamp.
An *ooky spooky* swamp.
What will we do?
We'll wade across!
Romp and *stomp*.
Romp and *stomp*.
Across the *ooky spooky* swamp.

We're going on a ghost hunt
to catch a trick-or-treat ghost.
We're not afraid.
No, we're not afraid.
No, we're not afraid at all!

Looking high.
Looking low.
Off on a ghost hunt.
Here we go!

Oh, dear. What have we here?
A haunted house.
A haunted house,
where goblins go thump.
What will we do?
We'll dash past.
Rumpety bump.
Rumpety bump.
Past a haunted house,
where goblins go thump.

We're going on a ghost hunt
to catch a trick-or-treat ghost.
We're not afraid.
No, we're not afraid.
No, we're not afraid at all!

Looking high.
Looking low.
Off on a ghost hunt.
Here we go!

Oh, dear. What have we here?
Bats.
Big black bats, all furry and fat.
What will we do?
We'll *scurry*
under.
Skitter and *scat.*
Skitter and *scat.*
Under big black bats,
all furry and fat.

We're going on a ghost hunt
to catch a trick-or-treat ghost.
We're not afraid.
No, we're not afraid.
No, we're not afraid at all!

Looking high.
Looking low.
Off on a ghost hunt.
Here we go!

Oh, dear. What have we here?
Skeleton bones.
Skeleton bones that dance about.
What will we do?
We'll fly by.
Run and *shout.*
Run and *shout.*
By skeleton bones that dance about.

We're going on a ghost hunt
to catch a trick-or-treat ghost.
We're not afraid.
No, we're not afraid.
No, we're not afraid at all!

Looking high.
Looking low.
Off on a ghost hunt.
Here we go!

Oh, dear. What have we here?
A cave.
A creepy cave,
where the old ghost dwells!
What will we do?
We'll crawl through.
Oh... so... slow.
Oh... so... slow.
Into the creepy cave we go.

"Uh-oh. Do you see what *I* see?"
"Is it a rock?"
"Does a rock have long arms?"
"Is it a bush?"
"Does a bush have a *twirling, swirling* body?"
"Is it a mossy log?"
"Does a mossy log have *big round* eyes?"
"I give up. What do you see?"

“A ghost.
A great big scary ghost!
Off we go!”

Oh so *slow.* Oh so *slow.*
Out of the creepy cave we *go*....

Run and *shout. Run* and *shout.*
By skeleton bones
that dance about…

Skitter and *scat. Skitter* and *scat.*
Under big black bats,
all furry and fat…

Rumpety bump. Rumpety bump.
Past the haunted house,
where goblins go thump…

Romp and *stomp. Romp* and *stomp.*
Across the *ooky spooky* swamp…

Hurry. Hurry.
Fast, fast, fast.
Slam the door.
Safe—at last.

"I was looking for you!"

“We went on a ghost hunt
to catch a trick-or-treat ghost.
We weren’t afraid.
No, we weren’t afraid.
No, we weren’t afraid at all!”